Mrs Reinhardt

EDNA O'BRIEN

A Phoenix Paperback

Number Ten originally appeared in a slightly different form in
The New Yorker.
Both stories taken from *Mrs Reinhardt & Other Stories*
published by George Weidenfeld & Nicolson Ltd, 1978 and 1990

This edition published in 1996 by Phoenix
a division of Orion Books Ltd
Orion House, 5 Upper St Martin's Lane, London WC2H 9EA

ISBN 1 85799 767 0

Typeset by Deltatype Ltd, Ellesmere Port, Cheshire
Printed in Great Britain by Clays Ltd, St Ives plc

Contents

You who by love brought into
being delirium in my heart,
O Dion.

Plato

Number Ten

Everything began to be better for Mrs Reinhardt from the moment she started to sleepwalk. Every night her journey yielded a fresh surprise. First it was that she saw sheep – not sheep as one sees them in life, a bit sooty and bleating away, but sheep as one sees them in a dream. She saw myriads of white fleece on a hilltop, surrounded by little lambs frisking and suckling to their hearts' content.

Then she saw pictures such as she had not seen in life. Her husband owned an art gallery and Mrs Reinhardt had the opportunity to see many pictures, yet the ones she saw at night were much more satisfying. For one thing she was inside them. She was not an outsider looking in, making idiotic remarks, she was part of the picture: an arm or a lily or the grey mane of a horse. She did not have to compete, did not have to say anything. All her movements were preordained. She was simply aware of her own breath, a soft steady, sustaining breath.

In the mornings her husband would say she looked a bit frayed or a bit intense, and she would say, 'Nonsense,' because in fifteen years of marriage she had never felt better. Her sleeping life suited her and, of course, she never knew what to expect. Her daily life had a pattern to it. Weekday mornings she spent at home, helping or supervising Fatima, the Spanish maid. She gave two afternoons a week to teaching autistic children, two afternoons were devoted to an exercise class, and on Fridays she shopped in Harrods and got all the groceries for the weekend. Mr Reinhardt had bought a farm two years before, and weekends they spent in the country, in their newly renovated cottage. In the country she did not sleepwalk, and Mrs Reinhardt wondered if it might be that she was inhibited by the barbed-wire fence that skirted their garden. But there are gates, she thought, and I should open them. She was a little vexed with herself for not being more venturesome.

Then one May night, in her house in London, she had an incredible dream. She walked over a field with her youngest son – in real life he was at university – and all of a sudden, and in unison, the two of them knelt down and began scraping the earth up with their bare hands. It was a rich red earth and easy to crumble. They were so eager because they knew that treasure was about to be theirs. Sure enough, they found bits of gold, tiny specks of it, which they put in a handkerchief, and then to crown her happiness Mrs Reinhardt found the loveliest little gold key, and held it up to the light while her son laughed and in a baby voice said,

'Mama.'

Soon after this dream Mrs Reinhardt embarked on a bit of spring cleaning. Curtains and carpets for the dry cleaners, drawers depleted of all the old useless odds and ends that had been piling up. Her husband's clothing, too, she must put in order. A little rift had sprung up between them and was widening day by day. He was moody. He got home later than usual and, though he did not say so, she knew that he had stopped at the corner and had a few drinks. Once of late he had pulled her down beside him on the living-room sofa and stroked her thighs and started to undress her within hearing distance of Fatima, who was in the kitchen chopping and singing. Always chopping and singing or humming. For the most part, though, Mr Reinhardt went straight to the liquor cabinet and gave them both a gin, pouring himself a bigger one because, as he said, all her bloody fasting made Mrs Reinhardt light-headed.

She was sorting Mr Reinhardt's shirts – tee shirts, summer sweaters, thick crew-neck sweaters – and putting them each in a neat pile, when out of his seersucker jacket there tumbled a little gold key that caused her to let out a cry. The first thing she felt was a jet of fear. Then she bent down and picked it up. It was exactly like the one in her sleepwalk. She held it in her hand, promising herself never to let it go. What fools we are to pursue in daylight what we should leave for night-time.

Her next sleepwalking brought Mrs Reinhardt out of her house into a waiting taxi and, some distance away, to a mews house. Outside the mews house was a black and white tub filled with pretty flowers. She simply put her hand under a bit of foliage and there was the latchkey. Inside was a little nest. The wallpaper in the hall was the very one she had always wanted for their house, a pale gold with the tiniest white flowers – mere suggestions of flowers, like those of the wild strawberry. The kitchen was immaculate. On the landing upstairs was a little fretwork bench. The cushions in the sitting room were stiff and stately, and so was the upholstery, but the bedroom – ah, the bedroom.

It was everything she had ever wanted their own to be. In fact, the bedroom *was* the very room she had envisaged over and over again and had described to her husband down to the last detail. Here it was – a brass bed with a little lace canopy above it, the entire opposite wall a dark metallic mirror in which dark shadows seemed to swim around; a light-blue velvet chaise longue, a hanging plant with shining leaves and a floor lamp with a brown-fringed shade that gave off the softest of light.

She sat on the edge of the bed, marvelling, and saw the other things that she had always wanted. She saw, for instance, the photo of a little girl in First Communion attire; she saw the paperweight that when shaken yielded a miniature snowstorm; she saw the mother-of-pearl tray with the two champagne glasses – and all of a sudden she began to cry because her happiness was so immense. Perhaps, she thought, he will come to me here, he will visit, and it will be like the old days and he won't be irritable and he won't be tapping with his fingers or fiddling with the lever of his fountain pen. He will smother me with hugs and kisses and we will tumble about on the big foamy bed.

She sat there in the bedroom and she touched nothing, not even the two white irises in the tall glass vase. The little key was in her hand and she knew it was for the wardrobe and that she had only to open it to find there a nightdress with a pleated top, a voile dance dress, a silver fox cape, and a pair of sling-back shoes. But she did not open it. She wanted to leave something a secret. She crept away and was home in her own bed without her husband being aware of her absence. He had complained on other occasions about her cold feet as she got back into bed, and asked in Christ's name what was she doing – making tea or what? That morning her happiness was so great that she leaned over, unknotted his pyjamas, and made love to him very sweetly, very slowly and to his apparent delight. Yet when he wakened he was angry, as if a wrong had been done him.

Naturally, Mrs Reinhardt now went to the mews house night after night, and her heart would light up as she saw the pillar of the house with its number, ten, lettered in gold edged with black. The nought was a little slanted. Sometimes she got into the brass bed and she knew it was only a question of time before Mr Reinhardt followed her there.

One night as she lay in the bed, a little breathless, he came in very softly, closed the door, removed his dressing gown, and took possession of her with such a force that afterward she suspected she had a broken rib. They used words that they had not used for years. She was young and wild. A lovely fever took hold of her. She was saucy while he kept imploring her to please marry him, to please give up her independence, to please be his – adding that even if she said no he was going to whisk her off. Then to prove his point he took possession of her again. She almost died, so deep and so thorough was her pleasure, and each time as she came back to her senses she saw some little object or trinket that was intended to add to her pleasure – once it was a mobile in which silver horses chased one another around, once it was a sound as of a running stream. He gave her some champagne and they drank in utter silence.

But when she wakened from this idyll she was in fact in her own bed and so was he. She felt mortified. Had she cried out in her sleep? Had she moaned? There was no rib broken. She reached for the hand mirror and saw no sign of wantonness on her face, no tossed hair, and the buttons of her nightdress were neatly done up to the throat.

He was a solid mass of sleep. He opened his eyes. She said something to him, something anxious, but he did not reply.

She got out of bed and went down to the sitting room to think. Where would it all lead to? Should she tell him? She thought not. All morning she tried the key in different locks, but it was too small. In fact, once she nearly lost it because it slipped into a lock and she had to tease it out with the prong of a fork. Of course she did not let Fatima, the maid, see what she was doing.

It was Friday, their day to go to the country, and she was feeling reluctant about it. She knew that when they arrived they would rush around their garden and look at the rose leaves to make sure there were no greenfly. Then, staring out across the fields to where the cows were, they would tell each other how lucky they were to have such a nice place, and how clever. The magnolia flowers would be fully out and she would stand and stare at the tree as if by staring at it she could imbue her body with something of its whiteness.

The magnolia was out when they arrived – like little white china eggcups, each bloom with its leaves lifted to the heavens. Two of the elms definitely had the blight, Mr Reinhardt said, as the leaves were withering away. The elms would have to be chopped, and Mr Reinhardt estimated that there would be enough firewood for two winters. He would speak to the farm manager, who lived down the road, about this. They carried in the shopping, raised the blinds, and switched on the central heating. The little kitchen was just as they had left it, except that the primroses in the jar had faded and were like bits of yellow skin. She unpacked the food they had brought, put some things in the fridge, and began to peel the carrots and potatoes for the evening meal. Mr Reinhardt hammered four picture hooks into the wall for the new prints that he had brought down. From time to time he would call her to ask what order he should put them in, and she would go in, her hands covered with flour and rather absently suggest a grouping.

She had the little key with her in her purse and would open the purse from time to time to make sure that it was there. Then she would blush.

At dusk she went out to get a branch of apple wood for the fire, in order to engender a lovely smell. A bird chirped from a tree. It was more sound than song. She could not tell what bird it was. The magnolia tree was a mass of white in the surrounding darkness. The dew was falling and she bent for a moment to touch the wet grass. She wished it were Sunday, so that they could be going home. In London the evenings seemed to pass more quickly and they each had more chores to do. She felt in some way she was deceiving him.

They drank some red wine as they sat by the fire. Mr Reinhardt was fidgety but at the very same time accused her of being fidgety. He was being adamant about the Common

Market. Why did he expound on the logistics of it when she was not even contradicting him? He got carried away, made gestures, said he loved England, loved it passionately, that England was going to the dogs. When she got up to push in a log that had fallen from the grate, he asked her for God's sake to pay attention.

She sat down at once, and hoped that there was not going to be one of those terrible, unexpected, meaningless rows. But blessedly they were distracted. She heard him say, 'Crikey!' and then she looked up and saw what he had just seen. There was a herd of cattle staring in at them. She jumped up. Mr Reinhardt rushed to the phone to call the farm manager, since he himself knew nothing about country life, certainly not how to drive away cattle.

She grabbed a walking stick and went outside to prevent the cows from falling in the swimming pool. It was cold out of doors and the wind rustled in all the trees. The cows looked at her, suspicious. Their ears pricked. She made tentative movements with the stick, and at that moment four of them leaped over the barbed wire and back into the adjoining field. The remaining cow began to race around. From the field the four cows began to bawl. The fifth cow was butting against the paling. Mrs Reinhardt thought, I know what you are feeling – you are feeling lost and muddled and you have gone astray.

Her husband came out in a frenzy because when he rang

the farm manager no one was there.

'Bloody never there!' he said. His loud voice so frightened the fifth cow that she made a leap for it and got stuck in the barbed wire. Mrs Reinhardt could see the barb in her huge udder and thought what a place for it to have landed. They must rescue her. Very cautiously they both approached the animal, and the intention was that Mr Reinhardt would hold the cow while Mrs Reinhardt freed the flesh. She tried to be gentle. The cow's smell was milky, and soft compared with her roar, which was beseeching. Mr Reinhardt caught hold of the hindquarters and told his wife to hurry up. The cow was obstreperous. As Mrs Reinhardt lifted the bleeding flesh away, the cow took a huge jump and was over the fence and down the field, where she hurried to the river to drink.

The others followed her and suddenly the whole meadow was the scene of bawling and mad commotion. Mr Reinhardt rubbed his hands and let out a sigh of relief. He suggested that they open a bottle of champagne. Mrs Reinhardt was delighted. Of late he had become very thrifty and did not permit her any extravagances. In fact he had been saying that they would soon have to give up wine because of the state of the country. As they went indoors he put an arm around her. And back in the room she sat and felt like a mistress as she drank the champagne, smiled at him and felt the stuff coursing through her body. The champagne put them in a nice mood and they linked as they went up the narrow stairs to bed. Nevertheless, Mrs Reinhardt did not feel like any intimacy; she wanted it reserved for the hidden room.

They returned to London on Sunday evening, and that night Mrs Reinhardt did not sleep. Consequently she walked nowhere in her dreams. In the morning she felt fidgety. She looked in the mirror. She was getting old. After breakfast, as Mr Reinhardt was hurrying out of the house, she held up the little key.

'What is it?' she said.

'How would I know,' he said. He looked livid.

She called and made an appointment at the hairdresser's. She looked in the mirror. She must not get old. Later, when her hair was set she would surprise him – she would drop in at his gallery and ask him to take her to a nice pub. On the way she would buy a new scarf and knot it at the neck and she would be youthful.

When she got to the gallery, Mr Reinhardt was not there. Hans, his assistant, was busy with a client from the Middle East. She said she would wait. The new secretary went off to make some tea. Mrs Reinhardt sat at her husband's desk brooding, and then idly she began to flick through his desk diary, just to pass the time. Lunch with this one and that one. A reminder to buy her a present for their anniversary –

which he had done. He had brought her a beautiful ring with a sphinx on it.

Then she saw it – the address that she went to night after night. Number ten. The digits danced before her eyes as they had danced when she drove up in the taxi the very first time. All her movements became hurried and mechanical. She gulped her tea, she gave a distracted handshake to the Arab gentleman, she ate the ginger biscuit and gnashed her teeth, so violently did she chew. She paced the floor, she went back to the diary. The same address – three, four, or five times a week. She flicked back to see how long it had been going on. It was no use. She simply had to go there.

At the mews, she found the key in the flower tub. In the kitchen were eggshells and a pan in which an omelette had been cooked. There were two brown eggshells and one white. She dipped her finger in the fat; it was still warm. Her heart went ahead of her up the stairs. It was like a pellet in her body. She had her hand on the doorknob, when all of a sudden she stopped in her tracks and became motionless. She crept away from the door and went back to the landing seat.

She would not intrude, no. It was perfectly clear why Mr Reinhardt went there. He went by day to keep his tryst with her, be unfaithful with her, just as she went by night. One day or one night, if they were very lucky, they might meet and share their secret, but until then Mr Reinhardt was content to leave everything just as it was. She tiptoed down the stairs and was pleased that she had not acted rashly, that she had not lost her head.

Mrs Reinhardt

Mrs Reinhardt had her routes worked out. Blue ink for the main roads, red when she would want to turn off. A system, and a vow. She must enjoy herself, she must rest, she must recuperate, she must put on weight, and perhaps blossom the merest bit. She must get over it. After all, the world was a green, a sunny and enchanting place. The hay was being gathered, the spotted cows so sleek they looked like Dalmatians and their movements so lazy in the meadows that they could be somnambulists. The men and women working in the fields seemed to be devoid of fret or haste. It was June in Brittany, just before the throngs of visitors arrived, and the roads were relatively clear. The weather was blustery but as she drove along, the occasional patches of sunlight illuminated the trees, the lush grass and the marshes. Seeds and pollen on the surface of the marshes were a bright mustard yellow. Bits of flowering broom divided the roadside, and at intervals an emergency telephone kiosk in bright orange caught her attention. She did not like that. She did not like emergency and she did not like the telephone. To be avoided.

While driving, Mrs Reinhardt was occupied and her heart was relatively normal. One would not know that recently she had been through so much and that presently much more was to follow. A lull. Observe the roadside, the daisies in the fields, the red and the pink poppies, and the lupins so dozy like the cows; observe the road signs and think if necessary of the English dead in the last war whose spectres floated somewhere in these environments, the English dead of whom some photograph, some relic or some crushed thought was felt at that moment in some English semi-detached home. Think of food, think of shellfish, think of the French for blueberries, think of anything, so long as the mind keeps itself occupied.

It promised to be a beautiful hotel. She had seen photos of it, a dovecote on the edge of a lake, the very essence of stillness, beauty, sequesteredness. A place to re-meet the god of peace. On either side of the road the pines were young and spindly but the cows were pendulous, their udders shockingly large and full. It occurred to her that it was still morning and that they had been only recently milked so what would they feel like at sundown! What a nuisance that it was those cow's udders that brought the forbidden thought to her mind. Once in their country cottage, a cow had got caught in the barbed wire fence and both she and Mr Reinhardt had a time of it trying to get 15 help, and then trying to release the creature causing a commotion among the cow community. Afterwards they had drunk champagne intending to celebrate something. Or was it to hide something? Mr Reinhardt had said that they must not grow apart and yet had quarrelled with her about the Common Market and removed her glasses while she was sitting up in bed reading a story of Flaubert. The beginning of the end as she now knew, as she then knew, or did she, or do we, or is there such a thing, or is it another beginning to another ending and on and on.

'Damnation,' Mrs Reinhardt said, and speeded just as she came to where there were a variety of signs with thick arrows and names in navy blue. She had lost her bearings. She took a right and realised at once that she had gone to the east town rather than the main town. So much for distraction. Let him go. The worst was already over. She could see the town cathedral as she glanced behind, and already was looking for a way in which to turn right.

The worst was over, the worst being when the other woman, the girl really, was allowed to wear Mrs Reinhardt's nightdress and necklace. For fun. 'She is young,' he had said. It seemed she was, this rival or rather this replacement. So young that she shouted out of car windows at other motorists, that she carried a big bright umbrella, that she ate chips or cough lozenges on the way to one of these expensive restaurants where Mr Reinhardt took her.

All in all she was gamine.

Mrs Reinhardt drove around a walled city and swore at a system of signs that did not carry the name of the mill town she was looking for. There were other things, like a clock, and a bakery and a few strollers and when she pulled into the tree-lined square there was a young man naked to the waist in front of an easel, obviously sketching the cathedral. She spread the map over her knees and opened the door to get a puff of air. He looked at her. She smiled at him. She had to smile at someone. All of a sudden she had an irrational wish to have a son, a son who was with her now, to comfort her, to give her confidence, to take her part. Of course she had a son but he was grown up and had gone to America and knew none of this and must not know any of this.

She need never have gone into that cathedral town but as she said herself, she had seen it, she had seen the young man painting, she had given a little smile and he had smiled back and that was something.

For the rest of the journey she remained alert, she saw trees, gabled houses, a few windmills, she saw dandelions, she passed little towns, she saw washing on the line and she knew that she was going in the right direction.

Her arrival was blessed with magic. Trees, the sound of running water, flowers, wild flowers, and a sense of being in a place that it would take time to know, take time to discover. To make it even more mysterious the apartments were stone chalets scattered at a distance throughout the grounds. It was a complex really but one in which nature dominated. She went down some steps to where it said 'Reception' and, having introduced herself, was asked at once to hurry so as to be served lunch. Finding the dining room was an expedition in itself – up steps, down more steps, and then into a little outer salon where there were round tables covered with lace cloths and on each table a vase of wild flowers. She bent down and smelt some pansies. A pure sweet silken smell, like the texture of childhood. She felt grateful. Her husband was paying for all this and what a pity that like her he was not now going down more steps, past a satin screen, to a table laid for two by an open window, to the accompaniment of running water.

She had a half bottle of champagne, duck pâté and a flat white grilled fish on a bed of thin strips of boiled leek. The hollandaise sauce was perfect and yellower than usual because they had added mustard. She was alone except for the serving girl and an older couple at a table a few yards away. She could not hear what they said. The man was drinking Calvados. The serving girl had a pretty face and brown curly hair tied back with a ribbon. One curl had been brought onto her forehead for effect. She radiated innocence and a dream. Mrs Reinhardt did not look at her for long but thought she has probably never been to Paris, never even been to Nantes but she hopes to go and will go one day. That story was in her eyes, in the curls of her hair, in everything she did. That thirst.

After lunch Mrs Reinhardt was escorted to her chalet. It was down a dusty road with ferns and dock on either side. Wild roses of the palest pink tumbled over the arch of the door and when she stood in her bedroom and looked through one of the narrow turret windows it was these roses and grassland that she saw, while from the other side she could hear the rush of the water and the two images reminded her of herself and of everybody else that she had known. One was green and hushed and quiet and one was torrential. Did they have to conflict with each other? She undressed, she unpacked, she opened the little refrigerator to see what delights were there. There was beer and champagne and miniatures of whisky and Vichy water and red cordial. It was like being a child again and looking into one's little toy house.

She had a little weep. For what did Mrs Reinhardt weep – for beauty, for ugliness, for herself, for her son in America, for Mr Reinhardt who had lost his reason. So badly did Mr Reinhardt love this new girl, Rita, that he had made her take him to meet all her friends so that he could ask them how Rita looked at sixteen, and seventeen, what Rita wore, what Rita was like as a débutante, and why Rita stopped going to art school and then he had made notes of these things. Made an utter fool of himself. Yes she cried for that, and as she cried it seemed to her the tears were like the strata of this earth, had many levels and many layers, and that those layers differed and that now she was crying for more than one thing at the same time, that her tears were all mixed up. She was also crying about age, about two grey ribs in her pubic hair, crying for not having tried harder on certain occasions as when Mr Reinhardt came home expecting excitement or repose and getting instead a typical story about the non-arrival of the gas man. She had let herself be drawn into the weary and hypnotising whirl of domesticity. With her the magazines had to be neat, the dust had to be dusted, all her perfectionism had got thrown into that instead of something larger, or instead of Mr Reinhardt. Where do we go wrong? Is not that what guardian angels are meant to do, to lead us back by the hand?

She cried too because of the night she had thrown a platter at him, and he sat there catatonic, and said that he knew he was wrecking her life and his, but that he could not stop it, said maybe it was madness or the male menopause or anything she wanted to call it, but that it was, what it was, what it was. He had even appealed to her. He told her a story, he told her that very day when he had gone to an auction to buy some pictures for the gallery, he had brought Rita with him and as they drove along the motorway he had hoped that they would crash, so terrible for him was his predicament, and so impossible for him was it to be parted from this girl whom he admitted had made him delirious, but Happy, but Happy, as he kept insisting.

It was this helplessness of human beings that made her cry most of all and when long after, which is to say at sunset, Mrs Reinhardt had dried her eyes, and had put on her oyster dress and her Chinese necklace she was still repeating to herself this matter of helplessness. At the same time she was reminding herself that there lay ahead a life, adventure, that she had not finished, she had merely changed direction and the new road was unknown to her.

She sat down to dinner. She was at a different table. This time she looked out on a lake that was a tableau of prettiness – trees on either side, overhanging branches, green leaves with silver undersides and a fallen bough where ducks perched. The residents were mostly elderly except for one woman with orange hair and studded sunglasses. This woman scanned a magazine throughout the dinner and did not address a word to her escort.

Mrs Reinhardt would look at the view, have a sip of wine, chew a crust of the bread that was so aerated it was like communion wafer. Suddenly she looked to one side and there in a tank with bubbles of water within were several lobsters. They were so beautiful that at first she thought they were mannequin lobsters, ornaments. Their shells had beautiful blue tints, the blue of lapis lazuli, and though their movements had at first unnerved her she began to engross herself in their motion and to forget what was going on around her. They moved beautifully and to such purpose. They moved to touch each other, at least some did, and others waited, were the recipients so to speak of this reach, this touch. Their movements had all the grandeur of speech without the folly. But there was no mistaking their intention.

So caught up was she in this that she did not hear the pretty girl call her out to the phone and in fact she had to be touched on the bare arm which of course made her jump. Naturally she went out somewhat flustered, missed her step and turned, but did not wrench her ankle. It was her weak ankle, the one she always fell on. Going into the little booth she mettled herself. Perhaps he was contrite or drunk, or else there had been an accident, or else their son was getting married. At any rate it was crucial. She said her 'hello' calmly but pertly. She repeated it. It was a strange voice altogether, a man asking for Rachel. She said who is Rachel. There were a few moments of heated irritation and then complete disappointment as Mrs Reinhardt made her way back to her table trembling. Stupid girl to have called her!

Only the lobsters saved the occasion.

Now she gave them her full attention. Now, she forgot the mistake of the phone and observed the drama that was going on. A great long lobster seemed to be lord of the tank. His claws were covered with black elastic bands but that did not prevent him from proudly stalking through the water, having frontal battles with some, but chiefly trying to arouse another: a sleeping lobster who was obviously his heart's desire. His appeals to her were mesmerising. He would tickle her with his antennae, he would put claws over her, then edge a claw under her so that he levered her up a fraction and then he would leave her be for an instant only to return with a stronger, with a more telling assault. Of course there were moments when he had to desist, to ward off others who were coming in her region and this he did with the same determination, facing them with eyes that were vicious yet immobile as beads. He would lunge through the water and drive them back or drive them elsewhere and then he would return as if to his love and to his oracle.

There were secondary movements in the tank of course but it was at the main drama Mrs Reinhardt looked. She presumed it was a him and gave him the name of Napoleon. At times so great was his sexual plight that he would lower a long antenna under his rear and touch the little dun bibs of membrane and obviously excite himself so that he could start afresh on his sleeping lady. Because he was in no doubt but that she would succumb. Mrs Reinhardt christened her The Japanese Lady, because of her languor, her refusal to be roused, by him, or by any of them, and Mrs Reinhardt thought oh what a sight it will be when she does rise up and give herself to his embraces, oh what a wedding that will be! Mrs Reinhardt also thought that it was very likely that they would only be in this tank for a short number of hours and that in those hours they must act the play of their lives. Looking at them, with her hands pressed together, she hoped the way children hope for a happy ending to this courtship.

She had to leave the dining room while it was still going on, but in some way she felt with the lights out, and visitors gone, the protagonists safe in their tank, secured by air bubbles, would secretly find each other. She had drunk a little too much, and she swayed slightly as she went down the dusty road to her chalet. She felt elated. She had seen something that moved her. She had seen instinct, she had seen the grope and she had seen the will that refuses to be refused. She had seen tenderness.

In her bedroom she put the necklace into the heart-shaped wicker box and hid it under the bolster of the second bed. She had robbed her husband of it – this beautiful choker of jade. It had been his mother's. It was worth ten thousand pounds. It was her going-away present. She had extracted it from him. Before closing it in the box she bit on the beads as if they were fruits.

'If you give me the necklace I will go away.'

That was what she had said and she knew that in some corner she was thereby murdering his heart. It was his family necklace and it was the one thing in which he believed his luck was invested. Also he was born under the sign of Cancer and if he clung, he clung. It was the thing they shared, and by taking it she was telling him that she was going away for ever, and that she was taking some of him, his talisman, relic of his mother, his relic of their life together. She had now become so involved with this piece of jewellery that when she wore it she touched her throat constantly to make sure that it was there, and when she took it off she kissed it, and at night she dreamed of it, and one night she dreamt that she had tucked it into her vagina for safety, and hidden it there. At other times she thought how she would go to the Casino and gamble it away, his luck and hers. There was a Casino nearby and on the Saturday there was to be a cycling tournament, and she thought that one night, maybe on the Saturday she would go out, and maybe she would gamble and maybe she would win. Soon she fell asleep.

On the third day Mrs Reinhardt decided she would go driving. She needed a change of scene. She needed sea air and crag. She needed invigoration. The little nest was cloying. The quack-quack of the ducks, the running water were all very well but they were beginning to echo her own craving and she did not like that. So after breakfast she read the seventeenth-century Nun's Prayer, the one which asked the Lord to release one from excessive speech, to make one thoughtful but not moody, to give one a few friends, and to keep one reasonably sweet. She thought of Rita. Rita's bright blue eyes, sapphire eyes and the little studs in her ears that matched. Rita was ungainly like a colt. Rita would be the kind of girl who could stay up all night, swim at dawn and then sleep like a baby all through the day even in an unshaded room. Youth.

Yet it so happened that Mrs Reinhardt had found an admirer. The Monsieur who owned the hotel had paid her more than passing attention. In fact she hardly had to turn a corner but he was there, and he would find some distraction to delay her for a moment, so as he could gaze upon her. First it was a hare running through the undergrowth, then it was his dog following some ducks, then it was the electricity van coming to mend the telephone cable. The dreaded telephone. She was pleased that it was out of order. She was also pleased that she was still attractive and there was no denying but that Mrs Reinhardt could bewitch people. It was when judging a young person's art exhibition that he met Rita. Rita's work was the worst, and realising this she had torn it up in a tantrum. He came home and told Mrs Reinhardt and said how sorry he had felt for her but how plucky she had been. It was February the twenty-second. The following day two things happened – he bought several silk shirts and he proposed they go to Paris for a weekend.

'If only I could turn the key on it and close the door and come back when I am an old woman, if only I could do that.' So Mrs Reinhardt said to herself as she drove away from the green nest, from the singing birds and the hovering midges, from the rich hollandaise sauces and the quilted bed, from the overwhelming comfort of it all. Indeed she thought she may have suffocated her husband in the very same way. For though Mrs Reinhardt was cold to others, distant in her relationships with men and women, this was not her true nature, this was something she had built up, a screen of reserve to shelter her fear. She was sentimental at home and used to do a million things for Mr Reinhardt to please him, and to pander to him. She used to warm his side of the bed while he was still undressing, or looking at a drawing he had just bought, or even pacing the room. The pacing had grown more acute. When she knitted his socks in cable stitch she always knitted a third sock in case one got torn, or ruined, while he was fishing or when he hunted in Scotland in August. She went just to be near him though she dreaded these forays. They were too public. House parties of people thrown in upon each other for a hectic and sociable week. The landscape and the grouse were the same wonderful colour – that of rusted metal. The shot birds often seemed to her that they had just lain down in jest so un-dead did they seem. Even the few drops of blood seemed unreal, theatrical. She loved the moors, the rusted colour of farm and brushwood. But the screeches of the dying hares and the dying stags pierced and then haunted her. They were so human. She cried one day up there on the crest of the mountain when those over-human sounds reached her. He saw it but walked on. It was a man's world, it was man's terrain, it was not the place for tears. She blew her nose and walked up. It was a good thing that the wind was so fierce and, also being busy at the hunt, the men were not searching faces for emotion. It was not like sitting down at dinner and flirting and making compliments.

She often thought that the real secret of their love was that she kept the inside of herself permanently warm for him like someone keeping an egg under a nest of straw. When she loved, she loved completely. As a young girl she was using a sewing machine one day and by accident put the needle through her index finger, but she did not call out to her parents who were in the other room, she waited until her mother came through. Upon seeing this casualty her mother let out a scream. Within an instant her father was by her side and with a jerk of the lever he lifted the thing out and gave her such a look, such a loving look. Mrs Reinhardt was Tilly then, an only daughter, and full of trust. She believed that you loved your mother and father, that you loved your brother, that eventually you loved your husband and then most of all that you loved your children. Her parents had spoilt her, had brought her to the Ritz for birthdays, had left gold trinkets on her pillow on Christmas Eve, had comforted her when she wept. At twenty-one, they had had an expensive portrait done of her and hung it on the wall in a prominent position so that as guests entered they would say, 'Who is that? Who is that?' and a flurry of compliments would follow.

When she turned thirty, her husband had her portrait painted and it was in their sitting room, at that very moment, watching him and Rita, unless he had turned it around, or unless Rita had splashed housepaint over it. Rita was unruly it seemed. Rita's jealousy was more drastic than the occasional submarines of jealousy Mrs Reinhardt had experienced in their seventeen years of marriage – then it was over women, roughly her own age, women with poise, women with husbands, women with guile, women who made a career of straying but were back in their own homes by six o'clock. Being jealous of Rita was a more abstract thing – they had only met once and that was on the steps of a theatre. Rita had followed him there, ran up the steps, handed him a note and ran off again. Being jealous of Rita was being jealous of youth, of freedom and of spontaneity. Rita did not want marriage or an engagement ring. She wanted to go to Florence, she wanted to go to a ball, to go to the park on roller skates. Rita had a temper. Once at one of her father's soirées she threw twenty gold chairs out of the window. If they had had a daughter things might now be different. Four people might have sat down at a white table, under a red umbrella, looked out at a brown lake, whose colour was dunned by the overhanging trees and saplings. There might be four glasses, one with Coca Cola, one or maybe two with whiskey and hers with white wine and soda water. A young voice might say, 'What is that?' poitning to a misshapen straw basket on a wooden plinth in the middle of the lake and as she turned her attention to discern what it was, and as she decided that it was either a nest of swans or ducks the question would be repeated with a touch of impatience – 'Mam, what is that?' and Mrs Reinhardt might be answering. Oh my, yes, the family tableau smote her.

So transported back was she, to the hotel, and a united family, that Mrs Reinhardt was like a sleepwalker traversing the rocks that were covered with moss, and then the wet sand between the rocks. She was making her way towards the distant crags. On the sand there lay caps of seaweed so green, and so shaped like the back of a head that they were like theatrical wigs. She looked down at one, she bent to pore over its greenness and when she looked up, he was there. A man in his mid-twenties in a blue shirt with lips parted, seemed to be saying something pleasant to her, though perhaps it was only hello, or hi there. He had an American accent. Had they met in a cocktail bar or at an airport lounge, it is doubtful that they would have spoken but here the situation called for it. One or other had to express or confirm admiration for the sea, the boats, the white houses on the far side, the whiteness of the light, the vista; and then quite spontaneously he had to grip her wrist and said 'Look, look,' as a bird dived down into the water, swooped up again, re-dived until he came up with a fish.

'A predator,' Mrs Reinhardt said, his hand still on her wrist, casually. They argued about the bird, she said it was a gannet and he said it was some sort of hawk. She said sweetly that she knew more about wild life than he did. He conceded. He said if you came from Main Street, Iowa, you knew nothing, you were a hick. They laughed.

As they walked back along the shore he told her how he had been staying further up with friends and had decided to move on because one never discovers anything except when alone. He'd spend a night or two and then move on and eventually he would get to Turkey. He wasn't doing a grand tour or a gastronomic tour, he was just seeing the wild parts of Brittany and had found a hotel on the other side that was hidden from everybody. 'The savage side,' he said.

By the time she had agreed to have a crêpe with him they had exchanged those standard bits of information. He confessed that he didn't speak much French. She confessed that she'd taken a crammer course and was even thinking of spending three months in Paris to do a cookery course. When they went indoors she removed her headscraf and he was caught at once by the beauty of her brown pile of hair. Some hidden urge of vanity made her toss it, as they looked for a table.

'Tell me something,' he said, 'are you married or not?'

'Yes and no . . .' She had removed her wedding ring and put it in the small leather box that snapped when one shut it.

He found that intriguing. Quickly she explained that she had been but was about not to be. He reached out but did not touch her and she thought that there was something exquisite in that, that delicate indication of sympathy. He said quietly how he had missed out on marriage and on kids. She felt that he meant it. He said he had been a wild cat and whenever he had met a nice girl he had cheated on her, and lost her. He could never settle down.

'I'm bad news,' he said and laughed, and there was something so impish about him that Mrs Reinhardt was being won over.

On closer acquaintance she had to admit that his looks were

indeed flawless. So perhaps his character was not as terrible as he had made out. She used to press him to tell her things, boyish things like his first holiday in Greece, or his first girl, or his first guitar and gradually she realised she was becoming interested in these things although in them there was nothing new. It was the warmth really and the way he delighted in telling her these things that made Mrs Reinhardt ask for more stories. She was like someone who has been on a voyage and upon return wants to hear everything that has happened on land. He told her that he had made a short film that he would love her to see. He would fly home for it that night if only he could! It was a film about motorcycling and he had made it long before anyone else had made a film about it, or written a book about it. He told her some of the stories. Scenes at dusk in a deserted place when a man gets a puncture and says, 'What the hell does it matter . . .' as he sits down to take a smoke. She sensed a purity in him alongside everything else. He loved the desert, he loved the prairie but yes he had lived on women, and he had drunk a lot and he had slept rough and he had smoked every kind of weed under the sun, and he wished he had known Aldous Huxley, that Aldous Huxley had been his dad.

'Still searching,' he said.

'It's the fashion now,' she said a little drily.

'Hey, let's get married,' he said, and they clapped hands

and both pretended it was for real. Both acted a little play and it was the very same as if someone had come into the room and said, 'Do it for real kids.'

In jest, their cheeks met, in jest, their fingers interlocked, in jest, their knuckles mashed one another's and in jest they stood up, moved onto the small dance area and danced as closely as Siamese twins might to the music from the juke box. In jest, or perhaps not, Mrs Reinhardt felt through the beautiful folds of her oyster dress the press of his sexuality and round and round and round they danced, the two jesting betrothed people, who were far from home and who had got each other into such a spin of excitement. How thrilling it was and how rejuvenating to dance round and round and feel the strength and the need of this man pushing closer and closer to her while still keeping her reserve. On her face the most beautiful ecstatic smile. She was smiling for herself. He did slide his other hand in her buttock, but Mrs Reinhardt just shrugged it off. The moment the dancing stopped they parted.

Soon after they sat down she looked at her tiny wrist-watch, peered at it, and at once he flicked on his blue plastic lighter so that she could read the tiny black insect-like hands. Then he held the lighter in front of her face to admire her, to admire the eyes, the long nose, the sensual mouth, the necklace.

34   'Real,' he said, picking up the green beads that she herself

had become so involved with and had been so intimate with.

'Think so,' she said and regretted it instantly.

After all the world did abound in thieves and rogues and ten thousand pounds was no joke to be carrying around. She had read of women such as she, who took up with men, younger men, or older men, only to be robbed, stripped of their possessions, bled. She curdled within and suddenly invented for herself a telephone call back at the hotel. When she excused herself he rose chivalrously, escorted her through the door, down the steps and across the gravel path to the car park. They did not kiss goodnight.

In the morning the world was clean and bright. There had been rain and everything got washed, the water mills, the ducks, the roses, the trees, the lupins and the little winding paths. The little winding paths of course were strewn with white, pink and pale blue blossom. The effect was as of seeing snow when she opened the windows, leaned out and broke a rose that was still damp and whose full smell had not been restored yet. Its smell was smothered by the smell of rain and that too was beautiful. And so were her bare breasts resting on the window ledge. And so was life, physical well-being, one's own body, roses, encounter, promise, the dance.

She drew back quickly when she saw that there Monsieur was down below, idly hammering a few nails into a wall. 35

He seemed to be doing this to make a trellis for the roses but he was in no hurry as he looked in her direction. He had a knack of finding her no matter where she was. The night before as she drove back late he was in the car park to say that they had kept her a table for dinner. He had brought a spare menu in his pocket. The big black dog looked up too. Somehow her own whiteness and the milk-likeness of her breasts contrasted with the blackness of the dog and she saw them detached, yet grouped together in a very beautiful painting, opposites, one that was long and black with a snout, and one that was white and global like a lamp. She liked that picture and would add it to the pictures that she had seen during the years she sleepwalked. She sleepwalked no longer. Life was like that, you dreamed a lot, or you cried a lot, or you itched a lot, and then it disappeared and something else came in its place.

Mrs Reinhardt dawdled. She put on one dress then another, she lifted a plate ashtray and found a swarm of little ants underneath, she took sparkling mineral water from the refrigerator, drank it, took two of her iron tablets and by a process of association pulled her lower eyelid down to see if she was still anaemic. She realised something wonderful. For whatever number of minutes it had been, she had not given a thought to Mr Reinhardt and this was the beginning of recovery. That was how it happened, one forgot for two minutes and remembered for twenty. One forgot for three minutes and remembered for fifteen but as with a pendulum the states of remembering and the states of forgetting were gradually equalised and then one great day the pendulum had gone over and the states of forgetting had gained a victory.

What more did a woman want? Mrs Reinhardt danced around the room, leapt over her bed, threw a pillow in the air and felt as alive and gay as the day she got engaged and knew she would live happily ever after. What more did a woman want? She wanted this American although he might be a bounder. He might not. She would have him but in her own time and to suit her own requirements. She would not let him move into her hotel apartment because the privacy of it was sacred. In fact she was beginning to enjoy herself. Think of it, she could have coffee at noon instead of at nine thirty, she could eat an éclair, she could pluck her eyebrows, she could sing high notes and low notes, she could wander.

'Freedom!' Mrs Reinhardt told the lovely supple woman in the flowered dressing gown who smiled into the long mirror while the other Mrs Reinhardt told the lovely woman that the mirabelle she had drunk the night before was still swishing through her brain.

After breakfast she walked in the woods. Crossing a little plaited bridge she took off her sandals and tiptoed so as not to disturb the sounds and activities of nature. It was the darkest wood she had ever entered. All the trees twined overhead so that it was a vault with layer upon layer of green. Ferns grew in wizard abundance and between the ferns other things strove to be seen while all about were the butterflies and the insects. Mushrooms and toadstools flourished at the base of every tree and she knelt down to smell them. She loved their dank smell. The air was pierced with birdsong of every note and every variety as the birds darted across the ground, or swooped up into the air. This fecundity of nature, this chorus of birds and the distant cooing of the doves from the dovecote thrilled her and presently something else quickened her desires. The low, suggestive, all-desiring whistle of a male reached her ears. She had almost walked over him. He could see her bare legs under her dress. She drew back. He was lying down with his shirt open. He did not rise to greet her.

'You,' she said.

He put up his foot in salutation. She stood over him trying to decide whether his presence was a welcome or an intrusion.

'Amazing,' he said and held his hands out, acceding to the abundance of nature about him. He apologised for his presence but said that he had cycled over to see her just to say hello, he had brought her some croissants hot from the oven but that upon hearing she was sleeping he decided to have a ramble in the woods. He had fed the croissants to the birds. He used some French words to impress her and she laughed and soon her crossness was washed away. After all, they were not her woods, and he had not knocked on her bedroom door, and she would have been disappointed if he had cycled off without seeing her. She spread her dress like a cushion underneath her and sat folding her legs to the other side.

It was then they talked. They talked for a long time. They talked of courage, the different courage of men and women. The courage when a horse bolts, or the car in front of one just crashes, the gnawing courage of every day. She said men were never able to say 'finito'. 'Damn right,' he said and the jargon struck her as comic compared with the peace and majesty of the woods.

'You smell good,' he would sometimes say and that too belonged to another environment but for the most part he impressed her with his sincerity and with the way he took his time to say the thing he wanted to say. Before the week was out she would lead him to her bed. It would be dark and it would be unexpected, an invitation tossed at the very last minute as when someone takes a flower or a handkerchief and throws it into the bullring. She would be unabashed, as she had not been for years.

They stayed for about an hour, talking, and at times one or other would get up, walk or run towards the little bridge and pretend to take a photograph. Eventually they got up together and went to find his bicycle. He insisted that she cycle. After the first few wobbles she rode down the path and could hear him clapping. Then she got off, turned round and rode back towards him. He said that next time she would have to stay on the bicycle while turning around and she biffed him and said she had not ridden for years. Her face was flushed and bicycle oil had got on her skirt. For fun he sat her on the bar of the bicycle, put his leg across and they set off down the avenue at a dizzying speed, singing Daisy Daisy give me your answer do, I'm half crazy, all for the love of you . . .

He would not stop even though she swore that she was going to fall off any minute.

'You're OK . . .' he'd say as he turned the next corner. In a while she began to stop screaming and enjoyed the swoon in her stomach.

Mrs Reinhardt stood in the narrow shower, the disc of green soap held under one armpit when she saw a rose branch being waved into the room. As in a mirage the petals randomly fell. Which of them was it? Him or Monsieur? She was feeling decidedly amorous. He climbed in through the window and came directly to her. He did not speak. He gripped her roughly, his own clothing still on, and he was so busy taking possession of her that he did not realise that he was getting drenched. The shower was full on, yet neither of them bothered to turn it off. The zip of his trousers hurt her but he was mindless of that. The thing is he had desired her from the very first, and now he was pumping all his arrogance and all his cockatooing into her and she was taking it gladly, also gluttonously. She was recovering her pride as a woman, and much more as a desirable woman. It was this she had sorely missed in the last ten months. Yet she was surprised by herself, surprised by her savage need to get even with life, or was it to get healed? She leaned against the shower wall, wet and slippery all over and lolled so that every bit of her was partaking him. She did not worry about him, though he did seem in quite a frenzy both to prove himself and please her, and he kept uttering the vilest of words calling her sow and dog and bitch and so forth. She even thought that she might conceive so radical was it and the only other thought that came to her was of the lobsters and the lady lobster lying so still while all the others crawled over her.

When he came she refused to claim to be satisfied and with a few rough strokes insisted he fill her again and search for her every crevice. This all happened without speech except for the names he muttered as she squeezed from him the juices he did not have left to give. She was certainly getting her own back.

Afterwards she washed and as he lay on the bathroom

floor out of breath she stepped over him and went to her room to rest. She felt like a queen and lying on her bed her whole body was like a ship decked out with beauty. A victory! She had locked the bedroom door. Let him wait, let him sweat. She would join him for dinner. She had told him so in French knowing it would doubly confound him. She went to sleep ordering herself pleasant dreams, coloured dreams, the colours of sunlight and of lightning, yellow sun and saffron lightning.

He kept the dinner appointment. Mrs Reinhardt saw him from a landing, down in the little salon where there were lace tablecloths and the vases of wild flowers. She remembered it from her first day. He was drinking a Pernod. It was almost dark down there except for the light from the table candles. It was a somewhat sombre place. The drawings on the wall were all of monks or ascetics and nailed to a cross of wood was a bird; it seemed to be a dead pheasant. He was wearing green, a green silk dinner jacket – had she not seen it somewhere? Yes, it had been on display in the little hotel showcase where they also sold jewellery and beachwear.

The moment she went to his table she perceived the change in him. The good-natured truant boy had given way to the slightly testy seducer and he did not move a chair or a muscle as she sat down. He called to Michele, the girl with curly hair, to bring another Pernod, in fact to bring two.

Mrs Reinhardt thought that it was just a ruse and that he was proving to her what a man of the world he was. She said she had slept well.

'Where's your loot,' he said, looking at her neck. She had left it in her room and was wearing pearls instead. She did not answer but merely held up the paperback book to show that she had been reading.

'You read that?' he said. It was D. H. Lawrence. 'I haven't read that stuff since I was twelve.'

He was drunk. It augured badly. She wondered if she should dismiss him there and then but as on previous occasions when things got very bad Mrs Reinhardt became very stupid, became inept. He gave the waitress a wink and gripped her left hand where she was wearing a bracelet.

She moved off as languidly as always.

'You're a doll,' he said.

'She doesn't speak English,' Mrs Reinhardt said.

'She speaks my kind of English,' he said.

It was thus in a state of anger, pique and agitation that they went in to dinner. As he studied the four menus he decided on the costliest one and said it was a damn good thing that she was a rich bitch.

'Rich bitch,' he said and laughed.

She let it pass. He said how about taking him to Pamplona for the bullfights and then went into a rhapsody about past fights and past bullfighters.

'Oh, you read it in Ernest Hemingway,' she said, unable to resist a sting.

'Oh, we've got a hot and cold lady,' he said as he held the big wine list in front of him. The lobster tank was gapingly empty. There were only three lobsters in there and those lay absolutely still. Perhaps they were shocked from the raid and were lying low, not making a stir so as not to be seen. She was on the verge of tears. He ordered a unique bottle of wine. It meant the girl getting Monsieur, who then had to get his key and go to the cellar and ceremoniously bring it back and show the label and open it and decant it and wait. The waitress had changed clothes because she was going to the cycle tournament. Her black pinafore was changed for a blue dress with colours in the box pleats. She looked idyllic. Ready for showers of kisses and admiration.

'How would you like me to fuck you?' he said to her as she watched Monsieur pouring the wine.

'You have gone too far,' Mrs Reinhardt said, and perhaps fearing that she might make a scene he leaned over to her and said, 'Don't worry, I'll keep you.'

She excused herself, more for the waitress than for him, and hurried out. Never in all her life was Mrs Reinhardt so angry. She sat on the hammock in the garden and asked the stars and the lovely hexagonal lamps and the sleeping ducks to please succour her in this nightmare. She thought of the bill, and the ludicrous jacket, as she realised, also on her bill, and she cried like a very angry child who was unable to tell anyone what had happened. Her disgrace was extreme. She swung back and forth in the hammock cursing and swearing, then praying for patience. The important thing was never to have to see him again. She was shivering and in a state of shock by the time she went to her room. She really went to put on a cardigan and to order a sandwich or soup. There he was in her dressing gown. He had quit dinner he said, being as she so rudely walked out. He too was about to order a sandwich. The fridge door was open and as she entered he clicked it closed. Obviously he had drunk different things and she could see that he was wild. He was not giving this up, this luxury, this laissez-faire. He rose up and staggered.

'Round one,' he said and caught her.

'Get out of here,' she said.

'Not me, I'm for the licks.'

Mrs Reinhardt knew with complete conviction that she was about to be the witness to and participant in the most sordid kind of embroilment. Alacrity took hold of her and she thought, coax him, seem mature, laugh, divert him. But seeing the craze in his eyes, instinct made her resort to stronger measures and the scream she let out was astounding even to her own ears. It was no more than seconds until Monsieur was in the room grappling with him.

She realised that he had been watching all along and that he had been prepared for this in a way that she had not. Monsieur was telling him in French to get dressed and to get lost. It had some elements of farce.

'OK, OK,' he was saying. 'Just let me get dressed, just let me get out of this asshole.' She was glad of the language barrier. Then an ugly thing happened, the moment Monsieur let go of him he used a dirty trick. He picked up the empty champagne bottle and wielded it at his opponent's head. Suddenly the two of them were in a clinch and Mrs Reinhardt searched in her mind to know what was best to do. She picked up a chair but her action was like someone in slow motion, because while they were forcing each other onto the ground she was holding the chair and not doing anything with it. It was the breaking bottle she dreaded most of all. By then her hand had been on the emergency bell and as they both fell to the floor the assistant chef came in with a knife. He must have dashed from the kitchen. These two men were of course able to master the situation and when he got up he was shaking his head like a boxer who has been badly punched. He said he always hated frogs.

Monsieur suggested that she leave and go over to Reception and wait there. As she left the room he gave her his jacket. Walking down the little road her body shook like

jelly. The jacket kept slipping off. She was conscious of just having escaped indescribable horror. Horror such as one reads of. She realised how sheltered her life had been but this was no help. What she really wanted was to sit with someone and talk about anything. The hotel lounge was propriety itself. Another young girl, also with a rose in her hair, was slowly preparing a tray of drinks. A party of Dutch people sat in a corner, the dog snapped at some flies and from the other room the strains of music as there was a wedding in progress. Mrs Reinhardt sat in a deep leather chair and let all those pleasant things lap over her. She could hear speeches and clapping and then the sweet and lovely strains of the accordion and though she could not explain to herself why, these sounds made her feel enormously safe, made her feel as if perhaps she was getting married and she realised that that was the nice aftermath of shock. She reckoned that by now they would have got rid of him, and wondered foolishly if he would have to hitch-hike to his own hotel.

The principal excitement next morning was the birth of seven baby ducks. The little creatures had been plunged into the brown rushing water while a delighted audience looked on. Other ducks sat curled up on stones, sulking perhaps since they were so ignored in favour of a proud mother and these little daft naked creatures. The doves too fanned their tails in utter annoyance while everyone looked towards the water and away from them. She sat and sipped coffee.

Monsieur sat a little away from her dividing his admiration between her and the baby ducks. He flaked bread between his hands then opened the sliding door and pitched it out. Then he would look at her and smile. Speech was beyond him. He had fallen in love with her, or was infatuated, or was pretending to be infatuated. One of these things. Maybe he was just salvaging her pride. Yet the look was genuinely soft, even adoring. His swallow was affected, his cheeks were as red as the red poppies, and he did little things like wind his watch or rearrange the tops of his socks all for her benefit.

Once he put his hand on her shoulder to alert her to some new minutiae of the ducks' behaviour and he pressed achingly on her flesh.

'If Madame were to find out!' she thought and shuddered at the prospect of any further unpleasantness. She did not ask about the bounder but she did ask later for a glance at her bill and there indeed was the veston, the gentleman's veston for sixteen hundred francs. After breakfast she sat out on the lawn and observed the behaviour of the other ducks. They passed their time very amiably she thought, they doze a lot, then scratch or clean themselves, then re-doze, then have a little waddle and perhaps stretch themselves but she doubted that a duck walked more than a furlong throughout its whole life.

Then on beautiful crested hotel notepaper she wrote to her son. She deliberately wrote a blithe letter, a letter about ducks, trees and nature. Two glasses with the sucked crescent of an orange in each one were laid in an alcove in the wall and she described this to him and thought that soon she would be indulgent and order a champagne cocktail. She did not say, 'Your father and I have separated.' She would say it later when the pain was not quite so acute, and when it did not matter so much. When would that be? Mrs Reinhardt looked down at the cushion she was sitting on, and saw that it was a hundred per cent Fibranne, and as far as she was concerned that was the only thing in the world she could be absolutely sure of.

Going back to her room before lunch she decided to put on a georgette dress and her beads. She owed it to Monsieur. She ought to look nice even if she could not smile. She ought to pretend to and by pretending she might become that person. All the burning thoughts and all the recent wounds might just lie low in her and she could appear to be as calm and unperturbed as a summer lake with its water-lily leaves and its starry flowers. Beneath the surface the carp that no-one would cast down for. Monsieur's tenderness meant a lot to her, it meant she was still a person to whom another person bestowed attention, even love.

'Poor lobsters,' she thought and remembered those beseeching moves. When she opened the heart-shaped box in which the beads were hidden Mrs Reinhardt let out a shriek. Gone. Gone. Her talisman, her life insurance, her last link with her husband Harold gone. Their one chance of being reunited. Gone. She ran back the road to the Reception. She was wild. Madame was most annoyed at being told that such a valuable thing had been so carelessly left lying around. As for theft she did not want to hear of such a thing. It was a vulgarity, was for a different kind of premises altogether, not for her beautiful three-star establishment. She ran a perfect place which was her pride and joy and which was a bower against the outside world. How dare it, the outside world, come into her province? Monsieur's face dissolved in deeper and deeper shades of red and a most wretched expression. He did not say a word. Madame said of course it was the visitor, the American gentleman, and there was no knowing what else he had taken. As far as Madame was concerned the dregs of the earth had come into her nest and though it was a small movement it was a telling one, when she picked up a vase of flowers, put them down in another place, and put them down so that the water splashed out of them and stained the account she was preparing. This led to greater vexation. It was a moment of utter terseness and poor Monsieur could help neither of them. He pulled the dog's ear.

Mrs Reinhardt must ring her husband. She had to. There in full view of them, while Madame scratched figures onto the page and Monsieur pulled the dog's ear, Mrs Reinhardt said to her husband Harold in England that her beads had been stolen, that his beads had been stolen, that their beads had been stolen, and she began to cry. He was no help at all. He asked if they could be traced and she said she doubted it.

'A case of hit and run,' she said, hoping he would know what she meant. Perhaps he did because his next remark was that she seemed to be having an eventful time. She said she was in a bad way and she prayed to God that he would say 'come home'. He didn't. He said he would get in touch with the insurance people.

'Oh fuck the insurance people,' Mrs Reinhardt said and slammed the phone down. Monsieur turned away. She walked out the door. There was not a friend in the world.

Mrs Reinhardt experienced one of those spells that can unsettle one for ever. The world became black. A blackness permeated her heart. It was like rats scraping at her brain. It was pitiless. Phrases such as 'how are you', or 'I love you', or 'dear one', were mockery incarnate. The few faces of the strange people around her assumed the masks of animals. The world she stood up in, and was about to fall down in, was green and pretty but in a second it would be replaced by a bottomless pit into which Mrs Reinhardt was about to fall for eternity. She fainted.

They must have attended to her because when she came to, her court shoes were removed, the buttons of her blouse were undone and there was a warm cup of tisane on a stool beside her.

A presence had just vanished. Or a ghost. Had just slipped away. She thought it was a woman and perhaps it was her mother anointing her with ashes and she thought it was Ash Wednesday. 'Because I do not hope to live again,' she said but fortunately no-one seemed to understand. She sat up, sipped the hot tea, apologised about the necklace and about the scene she had made. She was uncertain how far she had gone. King Lear's touching of the robe of Cordelia sprung to mind and she asked God if the dead could in fact live again, if she could witness the miracle that the three apostles witnessed when they came and saw the stone rolled away from Christ's grave.

'Come back,' she whispered and it was as if she was taking her own hand and leading herself back to life. The one that led was her present self and the one that was being led was a small child who loved God, loved her parents, loved her husband, loved the trees, and the countryside, and had never wanted anything to change. Her two selves stood in the middle, teetering. These were extreme moments for Mrs Reinhardt and had she succumbed to them she would have strayed indeed. She asked for water. The tumbler she was holding went soft beneath her grip and the frightened child in her felt a memory as of shedding flesh, but the woman in her smiled and assured everyone that the crisis had passed which indeed it had. She lay back for a while and listened to the running water as it dashed and re-dashed against the jet-black millstone, and she resolved that by afternoon she would go away and bid goodbye to this episode that had had in it enchantment, revenge, shame, and the tenderness from Monsieur.

As she drove away, he came from behind the tree-house bearing a small bunch of fresh pansies. They were multi-coloured but the two predominant colours were yellow and maroon. They smelt like young skin and had that same delicacy. Mrs Reinhardt loved him and valued the moment. It was like an assuage. She smiled into his face, their eyes met, for him too it was a moment of real happiness, fleeting but real, a moment of good.

The new hotel was on a harbour and for the second time in four days she walked over boulders that were caked with moss. At her feet the bright crops of seaweed that again looked like theatre wigs but this time she saw who was before and behind her. She was fully in control. What maddened her was that women did as she did all the time and that their pride was not stripped from them, nor their jewellery. Or perhaps they kept it a secret. One had to be so cunning, so concealed.

Looking out along the bay at the boats, the masts, and the occasional double sails, she realised that now indeed her new life had begun, a life of adjustment and change. Life with a question mark. Your ideal of human life is? she asked herself. The answer was none. It had always been her husband, their relationship, his art gallery, their cottage in the country, and plans. One thing above all others came to her mind and it was the thousands of flower petals under the hall carpet which she had put there for pressing. Those pressed flowers were the moments of their life and what would happen to them – they would lie there for years or else they would be swept away. She could see them there, thousands of sweet bright petals, mementoes of their hours. Before her walk she had been reading Ruskin, reading of the necessary connection between beauty and morality, but it had not touched her. She wanted someone to love. As far as she was concerned Ruskin's theories were fine sermons but that is not what the heart wants. She must go home soon, and get a job. She must try. Mrs Reinhardt ran, got out of breath, stood to look at the harbour, re-ran and by an effort of will managed to extricate herself from the rather melancholy state she was in.

During dinner the head waiter would come, between each of the beautiful courses, and ask how she liked them. One
was a fish terrine, its colours summery, white, pink, green,

the colours of nature. She would love to learn how to make it. Then she had dressed crab, and even the broken-off claws had been dusted with flour and baked for a moment so that the effect was the same as of smelling warm bread. Everything was right and everything was bright. The little potted plant on the table was a bright cherry pink, robins darted in and out of the dark trees and the ornamental plates in a glass cupboard had patterns of flowers and trelliswork.

'A gentleman to see you,' the younger waiter said.

Mrs Reinhardt froze, the bounder was back. Like a woman ready for battle she put down her squashed napkin and stalked out of the room. She had to turn a corner to enter the main hall and there sitting on one of the high-backed Spanish-type chairs was her husband, Mr Reinhardt. He stood up at once and they shook hands formally like an attorney and his client at an auspicious meeting. 'He has come to sue me,' she thought, 'because of the necklace.' She did not say why have you come? He looked tired. Mrs Reinhardt flinched when she heard that he had taken a private plane. He had been to the other hotel and had motored over. He refused a drink and would not look at her.

He was mulling over his attack. She was convinced that she was about to be shot when he put his hand in his pocket and drew the thing out. She did not mind being shot but thought irritionally of the mess on the beautiful Spanish furniture.

'They found it,' he said as he produced the necklace and laid it on the table between them. It lay like a snake as in a painting, coiled in order to strike. Yet the sight of it filled her with tears and she blubbered out about the bounder, and how she had met him and how he had used her and suddenly she realised that she was telling him something that he had no inkling of.

'The maid took them,' he said and she saw the little maid with the brown curly hair dressed for the tournament and now she could have plucked her tongue out, for having divulged the tale of the bounder.

'Was she sacked?' she asked.

He did not know. He thought not.

'Fine place they have,' he said, referring to the lake and the windmills.

'This also is lovely,' she said and went on to talk about the view from the dining room, and the light which was so searing, so white, so unavoidable. Just like their predicament. In a minute he would get up and go. If only she had not told him about the bounder. If only she had let him say why he had come. She had closed the last door.

'How have you been?' he said.

'Well,' she said, but the nerve in her lower jaw would not keep still and without intending it and without in any way wanting it to happen Mrs Reinhardt burst into tears, much to the astonishment of the young waiter who was waiting to take an order, as he thought, for a drink.

'He tried to blackmail me,' she said and then immediately denied it.

Her husband was looking at her very quietly and she was not sure if there was any sympathy left in him. She thought, 'If he walks out now it will be catastrophic,' and again she thought of the few lobsters who were left in the tank and who were motionless with grief.

'There is us and there is people like him,' Mr Reinhardt said, and though she had not told the whole story he sensed the gravity of it. He said that if she did not mind he would stay and that since he was hungry and since it was late might they not go in to dinner. She looked at him and her eyes were probably drenched.

'Us and people like him!' she said.

Mr Reinhardt nodded.

'And Rita?' Mrs Reinhardt said.

He waited. He looked about. He was by no means at ease.

'She is one of us,' he said and then qualified it. 'Or she could be, if she meets the right man.'

His expression warned Mrs Reinhardt to pry no further. She linked him as they went in to dinner.

*

The wind rustled through the chimney and some soot fell on a bouquet of flowers. She saw that. She heard that. She squeezed his arm. They sat opposite. When the wind roars, when the iron catches rattle, when the very window panes seem to shiver, then wind and sea combine, then dogs begin to howl and the oncoming storm has a whiff of the supernatural. What does one do, what then does a Mrs Reinhardt do? One reaches out to the face that is opposite, that one loves, that one hates, that one fears, that one has been betrayed by, that one half knows, that one longs to touch and be reunited with, at least for the duration of a windy night. And by morning who knows? Who knows anything anyhow.

A Note on Edna O'Brien

Edna O'Brien is the author of seventeen books, including *The Country Girls, Lantern Slides* and *Time and Tide*, winner of the 1993 Writers' Guild Prize for fiction. Her latest novel, *House of Splendid Isolation*, is published by Phoenix.

House of Splendid Isolation

'The great Colette's mantle has fallen to Edna O'Brien – a darker writer, more full of conflict, O'Brien nonetheless shares the earthiness, the rawness, the chiselled prose, the scars of maturity. She is a consummate stylist and, to my mind, the most gifted woman now writing fiction in English'

Philip Roth

'Wise, moving, exciting . . . It could be called a thriller. It could, in the broadest sense, be called a political novel. It is certainly a work of art'

Scotsman 59

'A compelling marriage of poetry and violence . . . captures the dilemmas of a country's love for itself, and the acts of kindness and violence committed in the name of that love'
Sunday Express